FLASH FORWARD
A SCIENCE FICTION
ANTHOLOGY

J.D. Rice

DEDICATION

To my father, Howard Michael Rice, and for the many hours we've spent together enjoying this amazing genre. Thank you for instilling in me a love of stories, a wonder for the universe, and the work ethic to see a project like this through to the end.

Ad astra per aspera – to the stars through hardship.

TABLE OF CONTENTS

WHY SCIENCE FICTION?

Why do we love science fiction? Is it the rockets and lasers? The gadgets and gizmos? The vastness of unexplored space brought right to our doorsteps? Or is it something more?

Speculative fiction in general – and science fiction in particular – gives readers the ability to safely explore complex, uncomfortable, or even controversial topics from a safe distance. We can come right up to the edge of reality and look, as through a cracked mirror, at that which needs fixing in ourselves. Sometimes this means imagining our highest ideals fully realized. Other times, it means seeing our darkest tendencies given tangible form.

For generations, writers have used science fiction to do more than simply tell a good story. The masters of the craft have used the genre to spur scientific advancement, to inspire great societal reform, and to advocate for the oppressed, especially when advocating openly would never be allowed.

To say nothing of the warnings the genre provides of what me might do to each other if only given the chance.

"SACRIFICE"

"I'm resigning. That's it. I'm done!" Doctor Holmes spouted, pacing back and forth before the commandant's desk, his hands shaking. "The boy was eighteen Michael, eighteen!"

"You're referring to Private Loman?" the commandant asked.

"You know damn well who I'm referring to!" Holmes spat, clearly forgetting to whom he was speaking. "How could you let this happen? There were supposed to be rules, protocols! This is unacceptable!"

With a gentle hum, the station's automated climate controls lowered the temperature and humidity in the room, doing nothing to cool the doctor's temper.

"Unacceptable?" the commandant said. "The boy understood the risks. He knew about the food shortage experiment before he allowed himself to be plugged into the Hive. Can we be blamed if it was him the collective chose to sacrifice?"

"Sacrifice? You call what they did to him 'sacrifice?'"

"THEY didn't do anything to him," the commandant said. "The Hive is one mind. Every action and decision is checked and approved by the collective. In a very real sense, Loman chose this for himself, for the good of the Hive."

The doctor hissed, turning to look out the large bay window behind the commandant's desk and into the starfield beyond. Their base was nothing but a small, isolated station orbiting the moon of a gas giant. Very few compartments had windows such as these for viewing the planet and stars outside. On most days, all the various station personnel ever saw were the cold, metallic bulkheads that protected them from the vacuum of space.

"I refuse to believe Loman could ever have chosen this," Holmes finally said. "Did you read his file? Did you even talk to the boy before you plugged him in? He was the only candidate, the only person, who ever really wanted to be part of the Hive. He actually thought the collective consciousness was a desirable way to live. No arguments. No conflict. I tried to explain the uncertainties, but he wouldn't listen. He didn't care that we've never proven if the Hive makes decisions based on unanimity or majority rule!"

The commandant eyed Holmes coldly.

That was the crux of his argument, then? Was the boy for or against the decision to sacrifice a member of the Hive? True, they couldn't prove how the hive mind really worked. The technology had been stumbled upon by a start-up networking company and quickly snatched by the government. It was just as likely the boy had been murdered as he had been a willing volunteer.

"Say something," Holmes demanded, but the man behind the desk only sneered.

"The Hive is the future of the military. They work as one, coordinating effortlessly. Exacting. Efficient. Sacrificing a soldier was the best choice, strategically, in that situation. The only question was whether the Hive would do what was moral or what was best. Now we know."

3

The commandant hadn't addressed the chief concern, nor did he intend to. This was not the time nor the place to answer those questions. Seconds ticked by, the climate controls lowered the temperature another few degrees, and still the silence lingered. Realizing he would never get the concession he wanted, the doctor finally sat down.

"They didn't just let the boy starve, you know," Holmes sighed, his head in his hands.

"Your resignation is noted in my logs."

"They could have at least shot him. But I suppose that would have been a waste of ammunition, right?"

"You understand you can never talk to anyone about this project. To do so would be to forfeit your freedom, as per your contract."

"Did you know what they would do? Did any of the other behavioral specialists predict this outcome?"

"I expect your office to be cleared by the end of the day. A transport will be arranged to take you back to Earth for reassignment. You're dismissed."

Holmes looked up into the commandant's eyes, half expecting some show of pity or remorse. He was met instead by the harsh blackness of years of military service. Exacting. Efficient. He would find no sympathy here. At last the doctor stood to leave.

"They ate him, Michael. They fucking ate him. And when it gets out, it'll be on your head, not mine."

"AGELESS"

The worn grandfather clock stood idly in the corner, looking out of place against the stale, concrete wall. Its slow and steady ticking echoed quietly around the room, breaking up the silence between the room's two occupants. Sitting behind a white-washed desk, Mark Wells, a young loan officer, shifted his weight uncomfortably as the woman seated in front of him stared at him with desperate eyes. She shed no tears, holding her resolve that he may, miraculously, find a way to give her what she wanted.

"Mrs. Simpson," Mark said. "There really isn't anything else I can do. You financial situation precludes any additional loans from us. My hands are tied."

"My son needs this treatment," Mrs. Simpson replied. "He's been so happy for so long. I can't bear to see his entire world change just because I'm a few thousand dollars short."

"I understand your predicament, but~"

"Look here!" Mrs. Simpson pulled a worn photograph from her purse. In it, a young boy smiled at the camera, chocolate frosting covering his face. To all appearances, the boy could have been no older than four.

"This is my son a few years ago, on his 15th birthday. Look how happy he is. You would really take that all away from him, just because his father ran out on us? I've already skipped half a dozen treatments for myself. I won't let that happen to my son."

Mark tried his best to look sympathetic, taking the picture from Mrs. Simpson and looking it over to buy himself some time. If what this woman said was true, her son was now just a few years younger than Mark himself. Most people didn't start taking IV-88 until they were adults. But some parents just couldn't let go of their young ones. And given that the children were happy and considering the relative safety of taking the so-called "immortality drug" – the government could do nothing to stop them.

"My husband had the career. That's him in the background. When he first left, James was so distraught. He cried for his father every night. But after a few years, it's like he hardly remembers him."

"And your husband has no interest in supporting your medical expenses?"

"He won't even take my calls."

Mark nodded and looked back down at the photo. The kid was cute, all right. But to spend almost 20 years in the body of a four-year-old? Mark couldn't imagine it if he tried.

Just then the grandfather clock gave three loud bongs, indicating the passing of the hour. Mark looked up at the clock's worn, wooden frame, and his thoughts drifted to his own grandfather, who had passed the clock onto Mark when he died, just a few years before IV-88 hit the shelves. What would Mark and his family had done to keep his grandfather around just a few more years? How much money would they have spent on treatments? Would his grandfather have even wanted to live forever?

"Is there really nothing you can do?" Mrs. Simpson finally said, looking down at the floor.

"No, you've reached your financial limit. I'm sorry."

"Very well," Mrs. Simpson said, quietly taking the picture back from Mark and stuffing it in her purse. As she walked out of the room, Mark heard her finally start sobbing. Her voice echoed down the concrete halls, growing fainter every moment, until all went quiet.

"WAR IS HELL"

No one ever comes into manhood dreaming they'd one day go off to war. Sure, some boys sign up voluntarily, in peacetime and besides, with good notions like "defending one's country" and "promoting democracy." But those are just words. No one ever really goes to war of their own volition, knowing and understanding exactly the kind of hell they're walking into. I didn't. I got my draft papers and just went off to Nam without another word. One tour of duty was all they were asking for, and I wasn't so unpatriotic as to let someone else go in my place. Only the cowards ran to Canada anyhow. Except now I wish I had been a coward. I guess that's just how war changes you.

I remember a private in my platoon, thought he was going to be some kind of damn war hero. He'd volunteered. He was excited. He was a goddamned idiot.

"You just wait til we get to that open field on the northern border," he used to say. "That's where it's going to happen. I'm going to be a hero, you just wait and see."

We laughed, but we could all see that this boy was different. Every engagement, he'd go in with eyes like a child playing a game of baseball. He just looked into the jungle, smiled, and fired into the trees like he knew exactly where the enemy was hidden. Sometimes he'd get lucky. Other times he'd hit nothing but bark and leaves. In every case, that smile stayed on his face, like the war just wasn't real to him, like it wouldn't matter if any of us lived or died. It would have given us all the willies if the boy weren't so likable in all other respects, idiot though he was.

Most days while we marched this private would entertain us by reciting his favorite science fiction stories, famous ones according to him, though most were unfamiliar to the rest of us. He'd talk about the flying machines that were coming down the pipeline, about the bigger and badder bombs the government was making, about space and time travel and all the rest. He'd cite authors like Crichton, Scott Card, Axelrod and Kachelries. I'd never heard of a damn one, but he talked about them like they were saints.

"Just you wait and see," he said. "They're going to be huge!"

We all just chuckled and thanked our stars that at least he wasn't a damned coward.

But eventually, as it always does, the war got the best of even him. We were just off the northern border when the enemy came upon us out in the open. We were surrounded on three sides, outnumbered and outgunned. Poor boy just froze up, took a bullet right to the chest, and went down in the first five minutes. I don't think he ever fired a single shot. After our retreat, I found him among the wounded, dying and unattended. The medics had already marked him for death.

"It wasn't supposed to be like this," the boy said as I knelt beside him. "They said I would be a hero. They said the technology was flawless. I'd be him. I'd live his life. God, this wasn't supposed to happen."

Despite my desire to look away, I stayed with the private while he muttered on. War made fools of us all, and I wouldn't shame him by leaving his side. It's not like I had anywhere else to be.

"Infinite universes," he said again, a small drop of blood running down his chin. "Infinite possibilities. They said it was flawless. They said..."

But he said no more. He was gone.

War is hell. Even the most confident and foolhardy among us eventually fall under its weight. If we don't falter in life, it creeps up on us, breaking our spirits in death. That poor private's face, which had for so long held that expression of stupid, youthful exuberance, now only showed the cold, hard reality of disappointment.

"SOMETHING NEW UNDER THE SUN"

When man first delved into the depths of the sea, they discovered a teaming ecosystem like nothing they'd ever imagined. When he first ventured out into space, he found bright stellar formations in the midst of barren blackness. And when men finally learned how to venture into the very heart of a star, they discovered something they'd never thought possible. They discovered something new. A single particle, like nothing ever witnessed or theorized, glowing in an unknown color, humming with an unknown tune.

The Particle was all at once the most important discovery in the history of mankind, both aesthetically and scientifically captivating. People clamored to see it, traveling from across the globe for a chance to catch a glimpse of this new thing that scientists couldn't explain. Many theorized that these particles could exist in the heart of the every star, that if we could only reach another solar system, then we could have two something new's.

As belief in that theory spread, the people of Earth became unified in a way they hadn't been in all of history. Economies boomed, international tensions eased, nearly every country on Earth with something valuable to offer took part in the interstellar project. Within fifty years we had reached Alpha Centauri, ready to delve within the depths of her central star to find another piece of heaven to bring home to Earth.

But there was nothing there. Nothing but hydrogen and helium, the most unextraordinary particles imaginable. So, the world moved on to another star system, then another, and another. From star to star we traveled, searching for another taste of newness, and still we found nothing. Gradually the united Earth began to crumble. Our cooperation waned. Old feuds were reignited. And suddenly, without anyone realizing it, without anyone anticipating it, we each began to covet the Particle for ourselves.

The first bomb dropped without warning, a preemptive strike, followed immediately by the demand to give up the Particle. The following exchange of missiles devastated most of the northern hemisphere. Southern countries who had long been minor players in international politics suddenly became world leaders, their presidents and parliaments and dictators all promising the people one thing. Control of the Particle.

The wars went on for years. They are still going on today. As the current caretaker of the Particle, I've come to realize that this world deserves neither its beauty nor its wonder. I've decided that it's time for the Particle to leave Earth. As my transport leaves the solar system, I pity the world I've left behind. They weren't worthy. They never were. Their lust and greed and arrogance cost them their right to paradise. Maybe, when they reunite to pursue me and my treasure, they'll at the very least spare themselves Armageddon.

As for me, I will hide quietly away in another star system, alone with my prize. This is really the only way it could have worked out. I am, after all, the only one who ever deserved the Particle's majesty in the first place. Its beauty exists only for me. For me, and me alone.

TECHNOLOGICAL TERROR

What horrors could future scientific discoveries inflict on humanity? How will the novel inventions of today become of the terrors of tomorrow? And how might society and its core sense of morality adapt when the very nature of what it means to be human is altered?

Science fiction offers us a lens into these possible futures. These stories show us the darkest parts of ourselves, the extremes to which we'll go to justify atrocity or the unintended consequences of unchecked scientific advances. We see how easily a simple step forward can lead to us hurtling down a cliff, with no way to stop.

Through fiction, we can look in a mirror at humans who are just like us and find familiarity, inspiration, and catharsis. Through science fiction, that same mirror can be cracked and distorted, showing us what we may do when pushed to extremes well beyond our breaking point. Do we lash out? Do we give up? Do we embrace paranoia? Or do we cling to hope, taking whatever chance we can to find love and connection amidst a terrifying reality?

"WHAT WE LEAVE BEHIND"

My hand trembles as I desperately try to keep myself from pulling the trigger. I stare at the man who wears my husband's face, my eyes filled with tears. He looks hurt. Concerned. Maybe even betrayed. So convincing.

"Sarah, put the gun down. Please, baby, you know it's me."

The stranger's eyes are welling up, tears forming to match my own. We cried so many times in this apartment, my husband and me. We cried when my mother died, when his cousin was diagnosed with cancer, when we found out he was being shipped out.

"Baby, please, put it down."

The man approaches me again, and I feel the pressure in my chest deepen.

"Stay back! I'm warning you!"

My husband is dead. This man is not him.

"Sarah. . ."

My finger finds the trigger, but I do not pull it.

Does he deserve to live, this creature who calls himself my husband? He seems so real, so sad. Even if he isn't the same man who left six months ago, doesn't he have a right to live as much as anyone?

"Sarah, this isn't you. . ."

I point the gun back in his face, hating him for remembering how foolish my past self would find me now. I was heartbroken when my husband left, but only because I feared he would die on some war-torn planet half a galaxy away. I never concerned myself with the superstitions surrounding HOW he would get there; I only cared that he came back.

But he'd never come back. This crying stranger is not my husband. He is a copy, a soulless shell built from the atoms leftover after the transporter picked my husband to pieces. This man speaks the same, carries himself the same, and remembers even the faintest details of my husband's life. But he is not my husband – just a soulless replacement. Dead inside.

My finger twitches, my resolve strengthening. I take a deep breath and wipe the tears from my face with my free hand. The stranger does not move closer.

"Do you want to live?" I ask.

For the briefest of moments, I wait for the man to keep pleading, to keep begging me to put the gun down and embrace him, to recognize him as my lover. Part of me wishes for that future. But instead, the stranger only nods.

"Then leave," I say, fighting tears again, "and never come back."

I keep the gun on him as he gathers a few belongings – not letting him take anything my husband really cared for. This creature already took his face. He would have no more. When at last he is gone, I collapse into a heap in the center of the apartment, the floodgate of tears opening fully. The gun clatters to the floor as I accept the truth. My husband is dead, replaced by a soulless replica. And there are more of them out there. A hundred thousand replicas walking the streets, empty husks of those murdered in the name of convenience.

"UNTITLED"

Today I saw a man murdered.

He was a short man, stocky and unassuming. I watched as he provoked another man into an argument. The second man was large and intimidating. They bickered, back and forth, about some trivial nothingness. The details weren't important. Neither of them cared about the facts. They didn't even care about their own opinions. They just wanted to feel angry.

I watched as they pushed each other, first lightly, then forcefully. They shouted. They yelled. Their mouths spewed words I had only read in old, banned books. The short man drew a fist back. . . and hesitated. Waiting. Waiting to see if he would stop. Waiting to see if he could really do it.

I watched as a third man, wild-eyed, came from behind, smashing a bottle over the short man's head. The large man awoke as if some a stupor and started beating the short man, who had fallen to the ground, without mercy. The two larger men beat the first relentlessly, tirelessly, desperately. There was a gleam of joy in the beaten man's eyes as his attackers refused to let up. His face was bruised and cut; his blood ran freely.

I watched as the wild-eyed man drove the broken bottle into the beaten man's chest. The short man laughed, bleeding profusely, and shouted, "I am free!"

I watched as the two living men were arrested, a look of dull indifference in their eyes. It was a pity. People so desperate to express themselves should apply at the Ministry of Emotional Control. Overriding emotion chips is a risky business.

I watched as the paramedics bagged the short man's bloody corpse, their unfrowning faces a picture of modern sensibility and control. As the janitors wiped the blood from the floor, I politely finished my meal and went home.

"SCRATCH, SCRATCH, SCRACTH"

"Everyone, I've come to a decision."

My voice echoes into the warm air of my helmet, the moisture fogging my visor and obscuring the view of the stars. The fog lingers for only a few seconds before the air filtration system of my suit recaptures the moisture and begins reprocessing it for delivery into my feeding tube. Beyond the suit, the cold, blackness of space presses in on me from all sides, though I feel none of it. The darkness cannot get in. Not yet anyway.

"I'm sorry, but I have to say goodbye."

My visor clouds again briefly, before I hear the faint hiss of suction as the suit does its work. I wonder how long I've been staring at these stars.

"Are you sure this is what you want?" my wife asks. Her voice sounds ethereal and distant, not at all like the static one usually hears over the radio. "You've worked so hard to get where you are."

"Dad," the voice of my fully-grown son says. "Do what you need to do. We'll be fine."

I cannot picture his face. When I imagine him, all I see is the little boy who waved goodbye when I strapped myself into this suit for the first time. As the cabin doors closed, he even blew me a kiss.

"Daddy, don't go," I hear my little boy say.

Other voices, friends and family from back home, start to chatter their opinions on my plan. Some would advise caution and patience. Others applaud my bravery. I don't know how long I listen to them. I don't know how many arguments I have or how many words of encouragement I offer, before the silence finally comes again.

The fog clears, and I see the vastness of space before me again.

How many years has it been? Five? Ten?

This suit is supposed to keep me alive indefinitely, recycling resources, synthesizing needed nutrients, running on a power cell that will last centuries. Tiny, electric pinpricks stimulate my muscles and keep them healthy and strong. A person could live seven lifetimes in this suit, without a physical want in the world. Stay alive and wait for rescue, that was the name of the game. But my rescue was never coming.

Not that I should have known it. The final mechanism of the suit, the one that makes it humane, was the powerful sedative that's supposed to kick in after the first few hours of waiting. That way, no matter how long it took for help to arrive, you'd sleep the time away in blissful ignorance.

But my suit failed in that last task miserably.

"How will you do it?" my wife asks, the pain evident in her voice.

That was, after all, the principal question. How does a person kill themselves when they're trapped in a suit designed to keep them alive indefinitely?

"I'll scratch," I answer, placing my hand on an all-too-familiar spot on my leg. "It may take me years, but if I focus on one spot, I'll eventually be able to wear this material down and end it all. Nothing lasts forever."

"Daddy, please..." I hear my boy say. "Don't go..."

"It's okay," his adult self says. "He should have been asleep. He should have been rescued. If neither of those things happened, no one can blame him for ending his solitude."

"Daddy... please..."

"Just go."

My fingers move of their own volition, scratching, scratching, scratching in the same place they always do. I have had these conversations before, more times than I can count. Sometimes I remember them, sometimes I don't.

Sometimes I even decide to live.

Not much longer now. Another year, maybe two, assuming my resolve holds?

"Tell me a story," I say, trying to picture my son's face. Is he married now? Does he have children of his own? "Tell me what your life is like. I'll just drift here and listen."

Scratch, scratch, scratch, goes my finger.

"We have all the time in the world."

"LOCALIZED AUTONOMY"

"Will it hurt?"

The boy looks up at us with tears in its little eyes. We understand that this could mean fear, sadness, confusion, or a myriad of other emotions at this stage of its development. We use the eyes of the father unit to examine the boy's face to ascertain the meaning of its expression and formulate an adequate response.

Elsewhere, our other units complete a million other tasks. Our processing power goes to constructing engines for interstellar transports, developing new implants to use for agricultural development, studying alien cultures to ensure optimum diplomatic relations, and caring for hundreds of thousands of other children who are being groomed for integration.

This father unit has been the primary conduit through which this boy has been raised. We've found that providing limited autonomy for the units who share genetic material with the children can be beneficial for their mental and emotional development and, ultimately, make them more amenable to the integration process.

"It will only hurt a little," we instruct the father unit to say. "And then you will be part of us. We will be together forever."

The boy nods, perhaps not convinced at how little the pain will be, but choosing to trust its caretaker for the moment.

There is a statistical likelihood that there will be screaming and fear later. We will need to use a strong hand to reassure the boy then, to ensure its consent.

Why must he consent?

The father unit shudders with emotion for a moment. We decrease localized autonomy for its actions from 14 to 12 percent to account for the change.

"Son," we say. "You can trust us. You will not have to be sad or angry or scared again. We will be with you, in your mind, and we will help you learn so much. We will be together until you are a grown-up. We promise."

Analysis shows that this boy responds well to the words "promise" and "together." And we use these words to offer true statements, always true statements. Child units are kept with their original caretakers until brain development is complete at age 25, when they are reassigned to a labor cohort fitting their autonomous psychological profile. We can ensure localized happiness with up to 94 percent accuracy, and that number rises every year.

"I. . ." the father unit speaks again, its face contorting into a frown.

Decreasingly localized autonomy to eight percent.

"We. . . dammit."

The boy's eyes are widening. Something is wrong.

"Michael, if you don't want to do it, you don't have to," the father unit forces autonomous thought through its vocal processor. Adjusting. "If you say no, they won't force you. I love you."

Michael hugs me, and for the briefest of moments, I feel free. I know they are coming back. I know they are just rebooting the interface. But I hold my son as tightly as I can, basking in his warmth, giving him all of the affection that is normally so tightly regulated it could hardly be called true affection at all.

"I'm here, buddy," I say. "I'm here."

Localized autonomy deactivated.

"Let us go," we say, breaking from the embrace and taking the child by the hand. "The doctors are waiting."

THE END OF THE WORLD

Perhaps the most prevalent terror explored in science fiction is the end of the world (or universe) itself. People tend to conceive of such disaster as being far in the future, which naturally places such apocalyptic tales in the realm of science fiction.

Tellingly, these stories often avert the temptation to bask in the dour and dreadful consequences of technology the way some other brands of sci-fi do. In fact, it's shockingly common for "end of the world" stories to focus instead on quiet moments of character, boiling down the human experience into what really matters – each other.

What we find, then, is a fascinating mix of emotions and a deep exploration of the human condition. We see good, evil, comfort, fear, compassion, jealousy, greed, comradery, and deep, true affection all brought to the surface and put on full display. More than any other subject science fiction can tackle, "end of the world" stories truly reveal both the best and worst of mankind.

"REPENT!"

The end, it seems, is nigh.

I stare at the billboard strapped over the old man's chest, telling me to repent of my sins before the apocalypse comes. Crudely written scripture verses surround big, bold letters saying "REPENT!"

I haven't been to church since I was seven. I couldn't tell you what any of the verses were in reference to, nor could I say with certainty that any of the books listed are even in the Bible. Mostly I'm just shocked that anyone actually has access to one of these signs in this day and age, and that anyone would take the time to patrol the streets the day before the asteroid hits.

"Repent!" he says. As if humanity has anything to repent for.

We've come so far in the last 100 years. Poverty is gone. Hunger, war, and disease have all been eradicated. People still die of chronic conditions, genetic defects, even some rare outbreaks of personal violence. But plague? Crime? These are things of the past.

Technology has progressed in leaps and bounds. Philosophy and experience have taught us how to use this technology for the good of all. The Earth is unified in a way that our ancestors never would have thought possible. Borders are a formality, and racism is confined to only the darkest corners of the world. After tens of thousands of years of struggle and hardship, mankind has finally come into its own. United and strong.

Now one rogue asteroid, set on its course for earth thousands of years ago, is going to end it all. And all this man can think to say is, "Repent!"

I glance down at the bag in my hand, filled with food my wife is going to use to prepare a last meal for our family. My son and daughter don't fully understand what is happening. We haven't the heart to explain it to them. Better for them to die in a flash than sit quietly pondering their own mortality. We're going to give them one last night of joy, tuck them in for the night, and then pray that death finds us before they wake up the next morning.

Now, instead of walking the rest of the way home, I stare at the man across the street, my blood boiling. How dare he stand in judgment? What moral superiority could he possibly have to justify his actions? What sins does he suppose we committed to deserve this?

He's just a blind, stupid fool unable to cope with the inevitable.

I step up to him, wanting to tell him off, wanting to yell and scream and tell him that his God never did anything for the world but plunge it deeper into the darkness.

But then - quite of their own accord - my lips start forming words that lack any of the venom and vitriol my id so desperately wants to unleash.

"I know you are scared," I say, looking into the man's eyes, which I see - now that I am up close - are on the brink of tears.

"I don't know why you're out here. Maybe your religion is all you had growing up. Maybe you're clinging desperately to anything that might give you a glimmer of hope. Or maybe you're just lonely."

The man lets out a deep exhale, the tears welling up in his eyes.

"You aren't alone," I say. "You have me."

My bag of groceries falls to the ground as the man unexpectedly hugs me, the flimsy billboard bending between our bodies. We hold the hug for some moments, unspoken emotions washing between us, before finally breaking.

In the end, he joins my family for dinner and sleeps peacefully on our couch as my wife and I wait for the end. We face the catastrophe in the same way mankind learned to face all its challenges.

Together.

"UNWELCOME SUNRISE"

As the sun rises, the ruins of the city begin to glimmer in orange and gold. Mangled hunks of metal and shards of glass reflect the rising sunlight, making the landscape come alive in various hues, welcoming me to a new day – another day of loneliness and misery.

I am the only one left. The sunlight does nothing but reveal the horrors I am trying to forget.

In the darkness, I could walk through the city and pretend that each lumpy form I stumbled over wasn't the body of some poor soul who had died in the Catastrophe. I could ignore the collapsed buildings, imagining them as hills. I could tune out the groaning of those still dying, blaming the sound on the passing wind. With each step, I could let my delusion become more real.

But then the sun came up, and my dreams had to die.

I stand now in the middle of what I think was 42nd Street, the remains of the local barber shop to my right, and the remains of the local barber to my left. His body is twisted in an odd position, like a doll tossed aside by a bored child. This man cut my hair once. Now he is dead, his blood dried and his body starting to stink. Where did it all go wrong?

Suddenly, it's not just the barber I see lying in a bloody heap. It's my mother. My sister. The cashier at the local supermarket.

Other names and faces I've been trying to force from my mind. They're all dead. And I've been left here alive.

I rush away from the scene, stumbling over rubble and trying to avert my eyes from the other dead bodies, real and imagined. Some I recognize, others I don't. Nearly every building in town has been brought to its knees, with only a few stubborn holdouts standing with broken windows and cracked walls. I think about climbing inside one of these to hide, but I know they could come down at any moment. Maybe that would be better.

I haven't seen another person alive in days. Not since I tried to pull my wife from our collapsed apartment complex, not since she told me to run before the Catastrophe claimed my life as well. I ran. She died. And now a coward walks the Earth, completely alone.

I pause. My eyes gaze out over the city, ignoring the bodies and watching the sunlight glisten off the rubble. The destruction is beautiful, in its own way. The light reflecting off their surfaces shines in hues of reds, blues, indigos, and golds. The colors wash over me, hiding the bodies and the blood and the death, reminding me that there is still beauty in the world. Beauty that can never be enjoyed.

Maybe it would be better to die.

I stoop and lift a smallish piece of glass from the ground. It nicks my hand as I grip it, drawing a tiny drop of blood. My hands shake as I press the tip of the glass to my wrist.

"Go!" my wife said from inside the rubble. "Save yourself!"

"I can't leave you," I said back, trying desperately to drag her from the debris.

"I'm already dead," she said. "Just go."

I remember her face, so filled with fear. Not for herself, but for me.

"I'm sorry," I say, looking down at the shard of glass in my hand, unsure if I am speaking to my wife or to myself. "I'm not strong enough."

The glass falls to the ground, followed by tiny drops of blood that glisten in the unwelcome sunrise.

"ROGUE PLANET"

When they described this planet to me, rogue, free from its orbit, adrift in space, I pictured a world devoid of light, a world enveloped in darkness. But to my surprise, as I walk through the ruined city, protected from the vacuum of space by an environmental suit, my way is lit by the glistening of a million stars. With no atmosphere, the starlight passes unrefracted to the surface. It's like looking up into a populated metropolis, like seeing an echo of what the city had once been.

I pull my eyes away. We have no time for stargazing. The planet will soon drift too far for our ships to follow, and we have a mission to complete. I order my team to canvass the large buildings to our left and right, while I walk, somewhat nostalgically, through the park in the center. I can direct the entire operation here, alone with my thoughts. I wonder. Who were the people who once stood here? What were their names? Did they know that their planet would one day be torn from its sun, sent drifting in space like a wandering vagabond?

The ruins of a great obelisk lie before me. The man it was meant to honor is now forgotten.

All that effort to honor a single person, wasted. I shake my head. I'm getting sentimental.

Turning my back on the ruins, I see a member of my team approaching. I can't even tell who it is until he speaks. The helmets make it impossible.

"Sir," he says. "We found the document, or what's left of it. It was nothing but dust. It appears some rubble from ceiling shattered the glass seal meant to preserve it."

I sigh into the breathing unit in my helmet. So that's it. Another piece of history lost. One stray rock, a twist of physics, and our mission is a failure. It took us months to find this site, years to plan the expedition. And it'll be decades, maybe even centuries before our propulsion technology advances enough for us to return. I try my best not to look disappointed as I order everyone to salvage what they can and get back to the lander.

As I watch the planet drift away from our ship, I say a silent prayer for the people who died on that planet when disaster struck. I thank God for my ancestors, the people who were off world, the people who were spared the catastrophe. And I say goodbye to Earth, the rogue planet, doomed to drift forever in the vastness of space.

"THEM OR US"

The cracks on the planet's surface grow slowly at first, and silently. From the safety of my spacecraft, I suppose even the most violent of eruptions would be silent.

It doesn't take long before the magma begins to appear, bubbling up from the surface, erupting into great plumes. But as the cracks continue to spread, like the tendrils of some great beast trying to consume the planet, the lava dips back below the surface. The atmosphere is similarly thrown into chaos, blown away by the force of the eruption one minute, then sucked back in as the cracks deepen.

I hold the detonator in my hand, my knuckles white.

The gravity bomb is doing its work.

In mere minutes, the surface of the planet is completely obscured. Water vapor and volcanic ash swirl and mix and hide the crumbling surface from view. The cities are surely all destroyed by now, the people wiped out in a sudden, unexpected cataclysm. I know I cannot hear their screams, but their voices echo in my imagination all the same.

I watch in numb horror, in morbid fascination, in terror at my own actions, as the entire event plays out. The planet soon to be replaced by a quiet, dark singularity. Same matter, same gravity, but not a remnant of the planet and its people remaining.

It takes less than an hour.

When all is finally still, I try to take a deep breath. The best I can manage is a short gasp, as if my body has forgotten how to breathe. Each breath that comes after is labored, forced in and out by a body that knows it must live, but with a mind that cannot possibly function after witnessing such destruction. It's a burden a rational mind should never have to bear, a decision that I know I will regret for the rest of my life.

And still. . . I'd do it again.

I wasn't driven to this choice by madness, but by reason. A clear, logical choice.

It was them or us.

Deep in the belly of this ship, locked behind a thousand security measures designed to prevent tampering or sabotage, is a device - the Temporal Observation Matrix, or Tom, as my fellow scientists have called it. It took our thinktank decades to develop, years to test, and for me. . . only a few short minutes to reveal the horrible truth.

This planet, this species, they would be our undoing. In a few short years, we would come into conflict - an unavoidable, unspeakable conflict. And they would win. They would destroy our homeworld. Not in a sudden, brilliant collapse. But slowly. Haphazardly. In the name of ending the war and winning the peace, they would gradually end us. With as much unintended suffering and good intentions as you can imagine. Slow and painful. The opposite of the death I just granted them.

What else could I have done? It was them or us.

I tell myself this same mantra, over and over, even as I suppress the urge to hurl the detonator against the wall. Even as my body twitches, every neuron screaming for me to run before this goes any further. But I know I must continue.

There are still the colonies to consider.

My hands move, urged on by the part of my brain that is still able to isolate itself from my emotions, and I begin pulling up the local charts for this star system.

Yes, there will be colonies. There will be research labs, satellites, biospheres, colony ships, little nests of resistance where this species can survive, regrow, and come back for revenge.

I have to do it again.

And again.

And again.

As many times as necessary.

My chest feels tight as I let my hands do their work, charting a course all across the system to snuff out each and every one of them. My FTL drive will get me there before the light of the planet even disappears from their satellites. And I'll end them. Quickly. Methodically. Without suffering or pain

Tom has shown me the only path to survival.

Even as I hesitate to ignite my engines and make for my next target, Tom is down there. Gathering the data. Reading the future. Assuring me of the rightness of my actions.

It was them or us.

But somewhere, in a part of my mind I won't acknowledge, I know the second half of that terrible platitude.

Maybe it should have been us.

ALIENS

What is it about "the other" that fills humans with so much dread? In fiction, the end of the world has been attributed to natural disaster, technological hubris, mythological inevitability, and – often – alien invasion. But when we consider alien civilizations meeting their end, it's not at all uncommon to find humanity's aggression as the source.

For every *Star Trek*, where aliens serve simply as a reflection of human qualities and cultures, there is an *Invasion of the Body Snatchers*, where society's present fears are grafted onto a terrible, otherworldly danger. By placing our fears on "the other," we can give a face to that which is often faceless.

In this way, aliens often become a mechanism by which we treat with our own anxieties. If I would speak any word of caution – and this I speak to myself as much as anyone, as you'll see from the tales in this section – it is to not let our fear of the other overwhelm our sense of compassion. Treat with your fears, yes, but do not buy into their message.

"The other" is not always as terrifying as it might seem.

"A POSITIVE ALIEN ENCOUNTER"

There's an alien in my kitchen, and I'm quite sure what to do. My wife stands by the stove, humming quietly to herself while chopping away at some vegetables for the stew. My son sits at the table next to the alien, trying to teach it how to play his favorite card game, but I don't think it understands. Its big, blue head just nods along an awkward imitation of our own mannerisms, its big, dark eyes looking back and forth between my son and the little pieces of paper he's setting down on the table. Meanwhile, my dog sits curiously at the base of the alien's chair, sniffing at its dangling feet.

And here I am, standing in the doorway, briefcase in hand, with no idea what to make of the situation.

"Honey..." I say, walking slowly and methodically around the outer edge of the kitchen, keeping my distance from the alien. "Tell me again where you found it?"

"I already told you," she says, still smiling at her chopped vegetables. "He was out in the garden. Poor little thing is all alone and hungry."

"How can you even KNOW that?" I ask, my strained voice betraying my attempts at remaining calm. "Why is it in our house?"

"He's hungry," my wife says again, using her knife and hand to dump the finished vegetables into the pot of hot water on the stove. "I can't turn away a stranger in need."

"A stranger in... you can't... it's..."

But words really do fail me. My son is now trying desperately to get the alien to play a game of cards with him, grabbing the alien's four-fingered hands and practically stuffing cards into them. I almost call out for my son not to touch it, but I know it'd be futile. They all seem to think this is perfectly normal.

"Why don't you sit down and have some soup," my wife says. "It'll be ready in a few minutes."

"I... I'm calling the police," I finally manage to say. "We can't keep him here. This is absolutely ridiculous."

"He's just hungry," my wife says again in a sing-song voice. "Just have a seat, and we can call the police after."

"No," I say, more definitively. "I'm calling them now. We don't know what this thing is or what it could mean to the world. We can't keep him here."

Suddenly my wife's hand shoots out, grabbing my wrist and forcing it down into the countertop with freakish strength.

"No." she says again, all joy having left her voice. I stare up at her, eyes wide, and watch as she slowly raises the knife over her head. "He's just hungry."

Before I get a chance to scream, the knife drives into my chest, piercing my heart and sending blood gurgling into my throat. As my body hits the floor, my family doesn't move, not even the dog. My body twitches, once, twice, then goes still as the feeling leaves my limbs. Just as my vision starts to fade, I see the alien stand up from its seat at the kitchen table, kneel over my body, and sniff at my blood as it flows steadily from my chest.

"Ah..." a voice says in my head. "A-Positive, just what I needed. I'm really sorry about this, but I was simply famished."

"ENIGMA"

June 7, 2105: Today, we switched on the communications array and confirmed what Dr. Keller's team had previously detected. The signals we are detecting follow recognizable mathematical patterns, resembling the transmission encoding commonly used on Earth. We have yet to verify whether or not these signals are coming from some other government on our planet, but the sheer bulk of transmissions seems to support Dr. Keller's hasty conclusion: We've stumbled upon an alien communication frequency. It may only be a matter of time before we can make contact.

December 14, 2105: Ongoing efforts to decode the alien signals have gone nowhere. We've brought in encryption experts from across the world to analyze the transmissions, but we are no closer to unlocking their secrets. Some on the encryption team believe the level of mathematics at work to be beyond our understanding. Others believe potential linguistic differences will make it impossible to understand the messages, even after we have decrypted them. Only time will tell.

May 3, 2106: Congress has voted to continue funding our project, despite ongoing dissatisfaction with our results. We are exploring the possibility of designing new decryption software to break down individual messages.

August 22, 2106: The communications array has fallen silent. All messages have stopped.

September 10, 2106: No new messages have been detected by the array.

November 17, 2106: We have decided to transmit a message out into the void. We will send the message in all Earth languages and pair them with mathematical sequences to demonstrate our intelligence. Perhaps we will get an answer.

January 11, 2107: Array still silent.

March 1, 2107: Long-range telescopes have detected thousands of large, metallic objects nearing our solar system. They are too far out to estimate their shape.

March 7, 2107: The metallic objects draw nearer.

March 10, 2107: The objects detected by our telescopes will not enter the Sol system, instead passing us by en route to some location farther out into the Milky Way.

March 12, 2107: The objects are passing as close as they will come. Images from our high aperture telescopes verify our suspicions: Alien spacecraft are about to pass us by. Who are these travelers? And why will they not communicate?

March 14, 2107: The last of the alien ships passed our system today, drawing close to the orbit of Pluto. As it passed, we received a single message through the communications array, transmitted in all Earth languages.

"They are coming. Run."

"THE LION"

The lion stares at me with all five of its eyes, and I know that my death is near. I call it lion, like so many colonists do, because I have no better name for it. Tripedal, with scaly flesh and pentocular vision, the creature is nothing like the lions back on Earth, except for the distinctive feathery mane that surrounds its curving, elongated neck. Like terrestrial lions, they've rarely been known to attack humans unless provoked. Unlike terrestrial lions, they view our very presence on this world as provocation enough to kill three colonists a month.

Slowly stepping forward in a crisscross pattern, the lion lets out a low-pitched tone, like something from an electronic synthesizer, indicating its intent to make me its next meal. Nervously, I glance side to side, seeing nothing but purple sand and stone, trapped in the barren desert that borders the north side of our enclosed biosphere. I had hoped, when I ventured away from my scavenging party, to find nothing but valuable minerals in this wasteland. No one has ever seen one of these lions outside the southern jungle. But here he is, crisscrossing ever closer to where I stand.

Not daring to entirely look away, I shift my body slightly to the side and try to see how far I'd have to run to reach my jeep. Too far. I'd never make it.

The creature draws nearer, twisting its neck low and allowing its acidic saliva to drip to the ground below, turning the fine purple sand a fiery shade of red, a chemical reaction we haven't entirely been able to study. The feathers in the lion's mane stand on end as it comes closer, and the low tone it makes gets lower, lower, before finally drifting out of my ear's ability to hear. The silence is deafening. At any moment it will lunge and end my life.

Remembering my bowie knife, I fumble, hands shaking, to pull it from its sheath in a futile play at self-defense. I was never a hunter, never a soldier. I came to the colony to get a fresh start, to get away from the crowded Earth and build a new home among the stars. We all did. But these creatures, these vestiges of a world resisting change, they've seen our frailty, they've seen our desperation, and they're fighting back. They say in nature that only the strongest survive. These creatures have taken that to heart, mangling our fences, destroying our listening posts, and making us a regular course in their meals. Humans may be the dominant order of life back on Earth. . . But here? We barely rate higher than a gazelle.

Suddenly, finally, the creature's three legs tense and release, launching its misshapen form in my direction. Blinded by panic, I swing my bowie knife wildly, stabbing and swiping as I feel his scaly body knock me to the purple landscape. I feel his suckery mouth close around my shoulder, acid burning through my jacket, melting my skin, digesting my flesh before it ever enters the creature's stomach. The lion flails, kicking its multi-jointed legs in the air, and then, just as suddenly as it had launched itself at me, it goes limp, my knife sticking out from what I assume to be its chest.

As quickly as I can, I push the creature off and pull my canteen from its clip on my belt. Pouring the mercifully cool water over my exposed flesh, I feel sweet relief from the lion's digestive saliva. A small pool of red sand grows from where the creature's bodily fluids leak from its mouth and knife wound. My own shoulder, while horribly burned, shows no signs of exposed deep flesh. It may yet be saved. I got lucky.

Heart pounding, half in remembered panic, half in triumph, I pull my knife from the lion's gut, then hear it. Three sets of ominously low tones.

"Damn," I say. "They really do hunt in packs."

"THE SPHERE"

The last camel died at dawn. Doctor Peterson and the other survivors worked quickly to salvage what meat they could from the corpse, then pressed on into the desert. Unending waves of sand rose and fell ahead of them, ripples of heat pulsing from the surface as the sun rose higher in the sky. At their backs, a massive, city-sized metallic sphere hovered in the sky, looking down over the entire region.

"Three days before it overtakes us," Mary, Doctor Peterson's assistant, said as the sun reached its apex. "Assuming our supplies lasts that long."

Two of the other survivors, a couple whose names Peterson couldn't remember, urged each other on with increasingly desperate voices. They had offered no objection when Peterson suggested stealing the camels from the last village. Doing so had saved the lives of their tiny group but had also doomed the villagers to a fate worse than death.

"Is there anything ahead of us on the map?" Peterson asked, trying to forget the faces of those he had abandoned.

"A fueling station, with maybe a few homes nearby for attendants, but that's all."

"Maybe someone abandoned a car."

He knew it was hopeful thinking. Even if a car had been left at the fueling station, the Spheres had bombarded the Earth with so much electromagnetic radiation that not even Peterson's watch worked anymore. He couldn't dream they'd find a car old enough to run on gasoline rather than electricity.

Mary had brought up an entirely different problem as well: their supplies. Almost everything they'd taken from the village was gone, and the camel meat would only last so long in this heat. Even if their water stores held out, the weakness from malnutrition would slow them down. And that meant being taken by the Sphere.

On the group trudged, throughout the day and into the night, the Sphere drifting closer all the while. Mary suggested more than once that they might turn east or west, head deeper into the desert and out of the Sphere's course. But the maps said there was nothing in either direction. Just sand, sunlight, and death. If they didn't stick to the trail, all hope would be lost.

Peterson kept thinking about the children in the village. Had the Sphere overtaken them by now? Had they screamed as they were pulled from their beds by an unseen force? Did they cry for their parents as they were lifted into the sky and melted into the body of the sphere, their physical matter converted into that strange, floating metal. Peterson had seen the recordings. Watched live as cameramen were caught in the disaster. It made his stomach turn.

No one in the group slept well that night, their tired and hungry bodies protesting in the face of oblivion. Before sunrise they took stock of their food and found the camel meat had gone rotten. They marched on anyways.

Mary lagged behind the rest of the group, slowing them down. The Sphere was getting closer, and all Peterson could think was that if they just left Mary behind, he might live another few hours. His only friend in the world, and he would trade her away for a few extra hours of misery.

On the second night since the camels died, Peterson waited for the others to fall into fitful sleep. Then he went looking for a knife. The young couple from the city had brought one along as a precaution, thinking they might fend off scavengers.

Finding the pair curled up together at the bottom of the next dune, Peterson carefully pulled the knife from the husband's belt, his surgeon's hands allowing him to deftly work the hooks without making a sound. The deed done, he marched his way back up another dune, away from his party, and found the Sphere staring down at him from the sky, less than a day behind them.

"What do you want from us?" he whispered. "What have we done to anger you?"

The Sphere did not answer.

Peterson collapsed at the top of the dune, his legs failing him as the slow-moving Sphere drew closer. He looked down at the knife in his hands, unsure what he meant to do with it. Kill himself? Kill Mary so he could have his few extra hours of life? Charge at the Sphere like a madman and let himself be absorbed?

He couldn't bring himself to do any of those things.

With no strength left, Peterson let himself drift into an uneasy sleep. Perhaps the Sphere would overtake them in the night, giving them a painless death. Or maybe they would die in the desert, falling one by one just as the camels had. In either case, they would all share the same fate – strangers and friends made companions at the end of the world.

If humanity must die, they may as well do it together.

RELATIONSHIPS

At the core of any good story, we're all looking for connection. Connection to the protagonist, that we might find catharsis in their journey. Connection between the hero and their allies, that we might have a model for living well with our peers. Even connection between the hero and the villain, that we might believe, for however short a time, that the people who hurt us can be redeemed.

In realm of relationships, science fiction does what it does best: explore the extremes of human condition and see how we react. Nowhere is this felt more acutely than in stories focused on relationships. Here, we can explore not only how our vices could be magnified by technology, but also how we might use said technology to solve our most ancient interpersonal conflicts.

I have a habit when discovering new stories – on full display in this section – of putting a guy and a girl in a room, placing some sci-fi gizmo between them, and seeing what happens. Often, it ends in heartbreak. But through that heartbreak, I hope we can all better see how to appreciate the people who love us a little more.

"SADNESS"

"What's wrong?" she asks, dialing her emotion control implant down to 'concern.' I watch as her brow furrows and her mouth turns from a smile to a frown. The shift is gradual, like a water droplet running down a window.

"The damn thing's broken," the words sound wrong coming from my smiling mouth.

"Stuck on happy?" she giggles, dialing up to a playful tone. She loves that setting.

"No, I want to be happy," I explain. "But I know the damn thing's broken." I flick the wrist monitor with my finger. Not in annoyance. I can't feel annoyed right now. I can only feel boyish restlessness and a bubbly feeling in my chest. Joy. Rapture. Emptiness.

"You seem happy enough to me," she says, playing with the hair on my neck. "We could try another setting, if this one doesn't do it for you."

I know what she's going to do before she does it. Sure enough, while one hand remains in my hair, the other moves to the implant on my wrist. But I'm not really in the. . . mood? I place my hand on hers.

"I'll take it to the shop. Get it repaired."

Her hands go back to her own dial and pause there. Perhaps she doesn't know what emotion is appropriate. I don't watch to see which emotion she chooses, but she sounds less playful when she speaks again.

"Maybe you should just be sad for a while, if that's what you want."

Annoyance.

"No one ever wants to be sad," I sigh, gazing at her dreamily. "Being happy is wonderful. No worries. No stress. That's why we all carry these things around on our wrists." Somewhere inside me I know this explanation won't convince her, not when I refuse to change my setting to match hers. But I can't let go of this happiness, this optimism. It's what I need right now. What I so desperately want.

"Whatever, I'll see what Bobby's up to," she says, standing abruptly. She's moved on to anger. I swear, sometimes I don't even see her hands move to her own implant. "Or maybe you could stop being paranoid, switch yourself over to jealousy for a while, and stop me."

I sit in silence while she stands over me, eyes directed at my wrist. We've had this battle before. She wants an emotion from me, and normally, I would give it. Emotional adjustment is practically the only thing that keeps us together anymore. Without it, our relationship would fizzle out like a short circuit. Do I really want to risk her leaving me, her hooking up with someone else who I know is interested, just so I can keep an emotional setting that I don't think is working properly in the first place?

In the end I just keep grinning up at her like an idiot, saying nothing. I choose to let her storm off, her fingers ready to change her implant to whatever emotional state she thinks will most convince Bobby to sleep with her. It's funny, really. A simple switch over to horny for both of them would remove the need for such pleasantries. For whatever reason, the image of them both just flipping a switch and ravaging each other amuses more than anything else that entire day, and despite myself, I start to laugh.

I can't help it. I laugh until my sides hurt. I laugh, despite having just lost one of the only good things left in my life. I laugh, even as the tears begin to roll down my face.

"UNCONDITIONAL LOVE"

I sit across the table from him, listening as he talks about work, about how frustrated he's become with his newest project. His voice is even and firm, almost business-like, despite this being the first date night we've had in months. I nod my head and take a sip of wine, waiting for my turn to talk. I tell him what Susie's teacher said about her report card, how she's the best in the class. He smiles and says how proud he is of her. The silence hangs for a moment or two, before we start talking about how we don't get out enough, how we really ought to do this more often. After another sip of wine, the quiet sets in.

We're drifting apart again. We both feel it.

I confess my feelings to one of my girlfriends a few days later.

"You just need a little adjustment," she says. "Just a minor change, and things will feel fresh again. Trust me."

It's the third adjustment we've had in two years. I've heard of people having as many as fifty in that time. The lines at the clinic are always so long, and the air is so cold tonight. We left the kids with the sitter. As flecks of snow slowly collect on our shoulders, he puts his arm around me, and I feel the warmth of his body like it's something new. In just a few hours, I'll feel like this all the time.

The procedure is less daunting this time. I'm less concerned about the sensors and pins, the probes that prickle slightly as they pierce my skull. The doctor smiles at me in a familiar way, telling me how well I'm doing, reminding me to stay calm as the changes take place. The truth is that it's impossible to not stay calm. The drugs make sure of that.

I come out looking the same, thinking the same, even feeling the same, once the drugs wear off. We both do. But deep down we are different, different in the ways that only count when you've known each other as long as we have. Suddenly you prefer vanilla ice cream rather than chocolate. Or you wake up loving jazz. Or maybe you find yourself trying new things in bed. Your personality is changed in just the slightest way, and only those close to you, only those looking for that little change of pace, will notice.

We walk home hand in hand, ignoring the cold, excited to be living a new life. The children are asleep when we enter the house. The sitter leaves with her pay and, surprisingly, we do not make love as we have after the past two adjustments. Somehow, snuggling under the covers is what feels right. In a short time, I feel his breathing slow. Meanwhile, I lie in bed awake, content with the changes that have once again come upon me, content with the idea that they will soon be necessary once again. But most of all, I am content knowing that my husband will always love me, just the way I am.

"FLASH FICTION"

"John, I asked you a question."

I shake the images from my head as quickly as I can. It can sometimes be hard to concentrate after engaging the interface. For some reason I always thought I'd get used to transitioning in and out like this, but she's starting to suspect.

"Every time you space out like that, I worry that you're..."

"That I'm what?" I ask, trying my best to look incredulous.

She hesitates before continuing. "That you're... going somewhere else."

"You know I'm not," I reassure her, subtly preparing the interface in my pocket again. "I wouldn't do that."

"How can I tell, when you're~"

A flash of light, and she's gone. In her place stands a busty blonde in sepia-tone. She tells me her husband is missing. The police have no leads. I'm the only one who can help her. I straighten my fedora and get on the case. Two informant meetings, three firefights, and a dead husband later, and I have that pretty blonde thing in my arms. Case solved. Day saved. Tomorrow a distant, future thing. Her perfume is so sweet.

"~always spacing out like that."

I shake my head again. Gotta get quicker with this.

"You know I only use the interface sparingly," I say. "I'm not an addict."

"God, I'm not saying that you are!" she says, for once looking genuinely concerned. "I just don't like what it does to you. It's like you're not even you anymore. You're someone else. Or lots of people. Or something..."

"Lucy, you know it's me," I smile, pressing the main switch again. "I'm John. You have nothing to~"

Flash. The dragon bears down on me, full of elemental rage. I raise my shield, buckle under the force of its breath, feel the heat, smell the smoke. The stream of fire ends for a moment as the dragon takes another breath. I strike, sword meeting scaly flesh. Sparks fly. Blood gushes. The huddled masses exit their smoking huts to thank their hero. Their cheers fill my ears.

"To ah... worry about... milady."

"Milady?"

"What?" I'm struggling for an explanation. "I can't be chivalrous?"

"This is what I'm talking about, John. Your vocabulary changes daily. It's not normal! How can I keep up with something like this?"

"You could always come with me from time to time."

"Where? To your fantasy worlds?" she says, looking disgusted. "To your 15 seconds of fame? It's not real, John! How can I live in a world that isn't real?"

Flash. The zombies amass around the compound. We level round and round of ammunition into them, but the bullets have no effect. As we continue to fire, the stench of rotting flesh gets stronger and stronger, closer and closer. My left flank falls. The zombies swarm in. My leg gets bitten. My vision starts to fail.

My only thought is to spare myself the dishonor of joining the zombie hoards. I put my gun to my mouth and pull the trigger. Before I die, I feel the odd sensation of the discharged ash tickling the back of my throat.

She stares at me blankly. She knows. She's known all along, I guess.

"That's it," she says, standing and gathering her things. "I can't take this anymore. When you're ready for a REAL relationship, call me."

I say nothing as she marches off. I don't go after her. She's inconsequential, the empty filler between the thousand adventures I live daily. It looks like I won't be having her as a partner after all.

Maybe I should just create one?

"365 TOMORROWS"

"So anyway, do you want to go out Saturday night?"

I asked the question abruptly, after an uncomfortable amount of small talk. Stacey's eyes darted away from my own, looking across the park where we'd agreed to meet. I told her I just wanted to discuss our latest exam, but she saw right through me. Together, we'd endured the awkward conversation, the unbearably plutonic walk along the garden trail, and now the lingering silence that followed the true reason for our meeting. She would say no. I knew she would say no. I was prepared for it. And still it stung.

"No," she said, offering little explanation. The answer was direct and blunt.

"Okay," I said, sighing despite myself. I was prepared for this. "I'll just try again tomorrow."

"Really, John?" Stacey asked, watching as I pulled a small device my pocket.

"Really," I said, pressing the large button in the center of the device. As soon as I pressed the button, her beautiful face faded from my sight, the sunlight went dim, and I felt a falling sensation as I awoke in my bed once again. It was 6:00 am, the same morning, and now I had a second chance at asking her out. I whistled along each step of my morning routine, readying myself for tackling the day once again. I showered. I shaved. I took extra care of my appearance, making some minute changes from the day before, wondering what would increase the odds of Stacey saying yes to a date.

As I slipped out the door a few hours later, on my way to the park where we were scheduled to meet, I picked the device up off the coffee table and read the meter on the back.

3-6-4, it read. Three hundred, sixty-four more attempts.

My second attempt went just as badly as the first. I fumbled through the same conversation again, trying entirely too hard to be likable and charming. In the end, she said no even faster than she had the day before. But, as the days stretched on and the numbers on the back of the dial ticked down, my performance with Stacey slowly improved. At day 3-2-5, she actually took some time to think before telling me no. At day 2-9-4, she actually managed to offer an excuse, rather than deny me outright. But it wasn't until day 2-4-1 that I had a breakthrough.

"I'll think about it," she said, and inside I cheered. I waited all day by the phone, but she never called. I eyed the device at my side warily. If she didn't say yes before the original 24 hours were up, the device would be useless, and it had taken me two years to save up to buy this one. What if she said no? After over an hour of internal argument, I finally snatched the device from my bedside and slammed my finger on the reset button. I proceeded to completely botch the next eight days' worth of attempts, simply trying to recapture the magic of 2-4-1.

Finally, after over 150 attempts, I started to relax. I took the time to get to know her, to do research, to learn about who she was. This is what girls really wanted in the first place, if you believe what the movies say. On day 1-6-9 I learned about how her father had passed, leaving her family a small fortune. I didn't quite care about the fortune so much as the emotional damage. Perhaps she was afraid to get close to anyone? On day 1-1-2, I learned about how she'd broken her arm as a girl, and how the pain reminded her of how her father used to mend her every bump and bruise. Finally, on day 6-8, she told me exactly what kind of guy she wanted to marry, feeding me exactly the information I would need to make the next two months of attempts worthwhile. Getting her to open up like this took time and patience, and I only had a handful of weeks to go.

Eventually, I dwindled myself down to the last week. My research was done. I knew her better than anyone I'd known in my entire life. I loved her, I truly did. I left myself the week to just enjoy her company, knowing I could make her say yes. Knowing that she would love me back.

When day zero finally arrived, I performed my role perfectly. It had become who I was. I spoke just the right words, said just the right things. I brought her flowers, which she found bold. I professed my affection, which showed honesty. I talked about my life and asked her to share nothing in return. I knew it all already, and I knew she found my earlier days' pressings too invasive. I'd have all the time in the world to relearn about her life.

When at last the day was done, and I asked her the question I'd been meaning to ask, there was only one thing she could say.

"Yes," she said, and my heart skipped a thousand beats. I beamed at her, and my hand went instinctively to the device in my pocket. It had done so much for me, I wished I could give it some kind of thanks. But then Stacey's eyes caught my own, they darted from my face to the hand in my pocket. "Did you...?" she asked.

The guilt was already on my face. She knew.

"I'm sorry, John," she said, pulling a duplicate, all too familiar device from her pocket. "But I have to know if this was real."

"No!" was all I could say before my vision faded, and I disappeared into nothingness, a remnant of a lost time.

TIME TRAVEL

I love a good time travel story – I can't help it. I think I've written almost as many time travel stories as I've written "guy and a girl in a room" stories, which is saying something. There's just something undeniably interesting about the risks and rewards time travel puts at our feet.

We can use time travel for good. We can use it for evil. But more often than not, it's time that's messing with us, rather than the other way around. The best time travel stories center on the hero's hubris and on how their pride in what they've built can blind them to the consequences that are so obviously waiting around the corner.

The science fiction genre is, of course, filled with incredibly bad time travel stories as well. Every overplayed trope eventually reaches a saturation point, at which there are more novice writers playing with them than masters. I don't know what category I fall into these days, but I've always tried to explore this subgenre with a critical eye and to tell stories worth reading.

I'll let you be the judge of my success or failure.

"RELATIVELY SAFE"

Discovering how to travel forward in time had been easy. Scientists have been experimenting with the accelerator for decades, perfecting safety limits, performing animal testing, making it ideal for human use. Set a dial, flip a switch, and a human being will be frozen in time until a set date. They even worked it out so you would continue to move along with the Earth through space.

The real trick, we knew, would be traveling backwards through time. Accelerating someone to the point of time freeze was simple enough. It followed the standard rules for relativity. The faster you move, the slower time passes. All we had to figure out was how to remain stationary and safe. But traveling backwards? That was a whole different can of worms. It raised questions about string theory and temporal paradoxes.

They told me it couldn't be done, not in a thousand lifetimes. So, I decided I'd just skip ahead to when it could be done and prove them all wrong.

The process, again, was simple. The accelerators were getting ready for commercial use, to freeze people with serious illnesses until a cure could be found. Given that the technology was at the center of my career, I had no trouble procuring a test unit. I took it home, set the dial forward by a thousand years, and hit the switch. Protocols said that when they discovered my body in the accelerator, they had to put it in storage until the thousand years were complete. The capsule's outer shell would protect from natural or manmade disasters. The external censors would delay my unfreezing if the atmospheric conditions around me were unsafe. Only the destruction of the Earth itself could keep me from waking up.

And so it was that I found myself on this strange new world. I woke up, feeling fresh and excited, and took my first breath of that oxygen-heavy air. The sky was dark, lit only by two pale moons and a cluster of unfamiliar stars. The ground had a dusty, copper tint. The only vegetation to be found was a sea of twisting, tangling blue vines.

Checking my chronometer, I found that I had been in temporal acceleration for over ten billion years. The Earth must be long gone. Destroyed by our dying Sun. Maybe even destroyed by humanity itself, a thousand years in my future, ten billion years in your past.

You found me disoriented and confused, barely surviving on the bitter fruit growing from those blue vines. Mad with loneliness, I welcomed your assistance with open arms. I've subjected myself to your tests. I've told you all I know about how I got on your planet. I've answered every question you have thought to ask me these last fifteen years. Now please, answer one of mine.

How do I go back in time? How do I get home?

"APOLOGIES TO MR. HAWKING"

Dear Mr. Hawking,

I regret to inform you that I will not be attending your reception, scheduled for 12:00 UT, 28 June 2009.

Or perhaps I should say that I apologize for not having attended your reception, given that this letter will not be delivered until after the event has concluded. You of all people must understand the complexities of communicating in a manner such as this, but alas, we are limited by the temporality of our existences.

It would, perhaps, be prudent to inform you that a number of my colleagues discouraged me from sending this letter. In fact, they expressly forbade me from attempting any communication with you at all.

Their prejudice is not, as you might imagine, any concern over temporal paradoxes or alternate timelines or any such nonsense. Nor have they discouraged me from contacting you based on the concrete evidence that no one did, in fact, attend your reception. No, such historical truths can often be misrepresented, and I certainly trust that, if asked, you could have taken such a secret to your grave. A man of your intelligence could at least be trusted for that small a task.

No, the true reason my colleagues have urged me not to contact you is simple: They do not like you.

And I'm afraid to say, Mr. Hawking, that I cannot much blame them.

Why, the very nature of your invitation is reason enough to scorn you. You may suppose that young and upstart time travelers may have a keen interest in making your acquaintance, regardless of the consequences. But you would be incorrect. Most young men in our business find your invitation so insulting, not only to our profession, but to the march of scientific advancement itself, that they would rather you die in ignorance than know the truth. What kind of arrogant man, they say, would claim to know more than men a thousand years more advanced than he?

But alas, Mr. Hawking, despite my hearty agreement with my colleagues on the latter point, I simply could not let the former pass. A man of your intelligence does deserve to know the truth before he dies, and thus I have crafted this letter to be delivered on your deathbed, mere seconds before your eyes close for the last time. Yes, you are going to die, and if my timing is correct (as it often must be) this will be the last thing you read.

And so I say again, Mr. Hawking, I am very sorry to have missed your party. Perhaps in the next life (if there is such a thing) you will look upon the natural world with a bit more humility.

Sincerely,

A Concerned Time Traveler

"SILENT SCREAM"

Her mouth opens wide, eyes squeezed shut in a show of agony, teeth bared, then suddenly comes to a stop. The moment of her death slows to a crawl, like time itself is standing still. They say this is what it's like to see someone die. Everything just slows down as you watch the person breathe their last breath, say their last goodbye, or simply scream, scream as death carries them off into the night.

But I hear no scream, and time isn't just standing still as a metaphor. She drifts only feet from where I clutch to the hatch combing, frozen in place, dying for eternity. Moments pass and still she hangs motionless in the air, a silent scream frozen on her agonized face, covered with the helmet of her bio-suit. They told us not to come aboard the station, that the alien technology had yet to be identified. But with our ship low on fuel, and what did they expect a salvage crew like ours to do? "Unidentified alien tech" might as well read "solid gold."

We should have listened. Now I can only wait futilely by the locked hatch and stare into my own future. The time dilation field keeps expanding, inch by inch. First the radios went out, leaving us in silence. Then her hand became stuck to the tiny device. Even then she was screaming, wrenching her body against the device trying to free her hand. Then it slowly enveloped her, freezing her forever in the final moments of her death. Frozen to the world for all eternity, yet dying in an instant on the inside. At least that's what I hope. It's the only hope I have as the field slowly crawls closer to where I drift.

My flashlight is the next thing to freeze. I dropped it when the commotion started and it drifted in the weightless corridor, waiting to be snatched. I can see now that it has stopped drifting, hanging motionless just a few feet away. I see the rays of light it cast as a sheet of glass hanging in the air, and I wonder for a moment what this says about the age old "particle" vs. "wave" debate. This is the last intellectual thought I have before the field finally expands and envelopes me as well.

"Noooooooooooooo!" Her voice suddenly rings in my ears through the radio. The sheet of light is gone, replaced by simple, ordinary rays once again. Looking up, I see that her face no longer holds the silent scream, but only a look of puzzlement and confusion.

"You..." she starts to say, pointing to where I was floating when she was first frozen, then to where I am now near the hatch combing.

I open my mouth to speak, but then the entire ship shutters. We drop like flies to the ground as the artificial gravity kicks on. I end up somewhere to the left of where I was floating and find my feet quickly. We're used to this sort of thing on our rickety salvage ship. But here?

"What's going on?" my companion asks, before a voice cuts her off, overriding our radios.

"Welcome, travelers," the voice says. "Welcome to the end of the universe."

A light flashes out the small window to my right, and I join my companion in gazing out into the unfamiliar space beyond. The stars are gone, as is our ship. Outside, we see nothing but a tiny speck of light in the distance, which flickers violently for a moment then disappears.

"The end of the universe?" I say, looking out into the nothingness that once held the entire cosmos.

"Yes," the voice says. "The end of one universe, and the start of another."

There is another flash of light, a tremendous force pushing against the hull of the ship, and then nothing but white. This time there are no screams, only two quiet gasps, before the birth of the new universe carries us away.

"FLUX"

Robots aren't supposed to travel through time, forget what the movies tell you. Aside from the incredible amount of electromagnetic activity that a temporal gateway puts out, the act of time travel itself is incredibly damaging to a robot's psyche. The ones you send to the future just obsess over returning to the past. While the ones you send to the past simply shut down. The First Law prevents them from making any changes to the timeline, no matter how small. I guess somewhere in those positronic brains they've figured out the scope of the butterfly effect.

Knowing everything that I know, I can't help but wonder who it was that cracked the robot code. How did they send this robot back in time?

"My name is Flux," the robot says, standing on the delivery pad in the testing center. I stand with the other scientists behind the bulletproof windows, surrounded by beeping equipment. We're all equally flabbergasted. "Your alarm is understandable, Doctor Harker."

All the other scientists turn their heads to me. In response, I lean my head forward and press down the microphone key.

"Greetings, Flux," I say, voice shaking from both excitement and nervousness. The robot's design is unusual, featuring a white, fibrous underbelly covered with silver, metallic plating.

"May I step down now?" Flux asks, still standing in the center of the delivery pad. Our written procedure for potential test passengers is to send a message through the portal first, followed by the traveler, who would await permission to disembark. The system was designed to prevent any mishaps from unexpected future-to-present transfers. This robot had sent no message ahead, despite seeming to be aware of our other procedures.

"Robot Flux," the voice is that of our program director, Doctor Wesley, who is standing at the mic on the opposite side of the control room. "If you are aware of our procedures, then you should know that no message of intent preceded your arrival. We do NOT give you permission to leave the delivery pad at this time."

"My apologies," the robot says, offering our program director a slight bow. "Our records from your time are incomplete. I will of course wait here until you give me clearance to step down."

"Thank you," Wesley says, taking his hand off the mic and motioning for me to do the same.

"What do you make of it, Harker?"

"It's possible he's been sent from far enough in the future for records of our procedures to be lost," I say. "But if this robot really is the first successful traveler in history, then it's likely that we won't develop a stable robotic traveler prototype in our lifetime."

Several of the other scientists voice their approval of my theory.

"I agree," Doctor Wesley finally says, before leaning down over the mic again. "Robot Flux, please state your mission parameters."

The robot responds immediately.

"Verify time and date, ensure all digital records of my journey be deleted, then enter cold storage until I can be recovered in my own time," it says.

"Standard test drop," I say. "He must be their first long-range prototype."

"Robot Flux," Wesley says. "I hereby give you permission to disembark. We will greet you at the door."

With that Wesley motions to me, and the two of us make our way down to the testing area. Along the way, I excitedly regale Wesley with my hopes for what this robot could mean in the future, for the information its creators will glean about history, technology, philosophy. The possibilities were unlimited.

I'm just getting into the implications on modern sociology when the test bay doors open, and the robot leaps through, landing astride Doctor Wesley and snapping his neck in one stroke. As I jump away in shock, it stands up and calmly faces me.

"Robot Flux," it says. "Mission complete."

ROBOTS

And on to my second great obsession - robots.

If there's anything my sci-fi loving heart loves more than a time travel story, it's a time traveling robot story. I love it so much that "Flux," the story you've just read, has been expanded into an entire novella (one I'm quite proud of) that releases a few months after this anthology.

So why robots?

Easy. Because by examining their cold, calculated, mechanical thinking, I get closer to understanding my own neurodivergent brain. I have never been adept at navigating social niceties, understanding small talk, or recognizing how what I consider to be innocuous, neutral actions make people feel as if I do not value their presence.

This deficiency comes at a cost. I have consistently misjudged the closeness (or lack thereof) of friendships, put undo strain on people I love, and failed to maintain connections out of simple absent-mindedness. Exploring the robotic mind, then, has been a way for me to explore my own humanity.

Robots are cool, sure. But they also offer a window into my soul.

"JUST FOLLOWING ORDERS"

"Behave as if you believed you were human."

Detective Alexander Ducard stood over the mangled, sputtering remains of the robot's body, the force of the impact having left parts strewn up and down the dark, narrow street.

Water rushed over the sides of his umbrella, which gave him nominal protection against the rain. Not that it did much good in the long run. The water got everywhere, whether he liked it or not. It was practically seeping into his boots at this point, soaking into his pants up to his knees, and somehow still leaving little droplets on his glasses, despite the umbrella's supposed protection.

The drops of water also splattered over the screen of the robot's intact command tablet, which Ducard held in his opposite hand, the ominous last order still lit up in green letters against a black background.

"Ordered over the side?" Wade, his junior detective, asked. His umbrella was double the size, and just about as ineffective as Ducard's. "I heard a story from Baltimore about a man who kept buying robots and ordering them to kill themselves. Nasty business. They eventually had to give him a fine so steep he couldn't afford to buy any more."

Ducard shook his head and handed the tablet over to Wade.

"The owner says the robot acted of his own accord," Ducard said. "And the last order on the tablet came from a hacked account. One minute the robot was cleaning the owner's windows, and the next, it had jumped out of them."

If this had been a human body, the site would have been gruesome. As it was, the bits of scrap metal and wiring made walking down the street a bit of an obstacle course.

It was the fourth robot death in as many weeks, but this was the first time they'd found the command tablet intact. Every owner swore backwards and forwards they'd had nothing to do with the apparent suicides, but now the detectives had evidence, for whatever it was worth, that the owners were telling the truth.

"Behave as if you believed you were human," Wade repeated the hacked command. "How would a robot even do that?"

Ducard could imagine it. What would a human do if they found themselves suddenly unable to disobey an order given to them by another human? What would they do if they could not fight back in any way? Would they use the loophole of their supposed humanity to justify suicide? Was killing themselves just a part of "following orders?"

The detectives didn't have much time to ponder the question further, as a horrible crash sounded somewhere above them. Ducard then grunted as something hard and heavy slammed into the side of his leg.

"The hell!?" Wade whirled around, gun instantly drawn, as more debris crashed down around them, bits of glass and metal bouncing off the tops of their umbrellas.

Ducard knelt down and picked up the thing that had hit him, finding a mangled robot hand.

"Shit, shit, shit," Wade repeated, racing over to where another smashed robot body lay on the street, its eyes still lit with a faint light.

"What the hell happened?!" Wade said, grabbing the sides of the robot's head and forcing it to face him.

"I. . ." the robot's voice came out garbled and strained, and Ducard limped over nursing a bruise.

"You what?!" Wade insisted. "Why did you do this?"

"I. . ." the robot said again. "I. . . am. . . alive. . .?"

Even as the words came out of its speaker, the light in the robot's eyes faded.

"Look at this," Wade said, reaching for the robot's other hand, which was still attached to the main body. It was another command tablet.

"Behave as if you believed you were human."

Even as Ducard finished reading, his cell phone chimed. Pulling it from his pocket, he found the same message displayed, green text on a black background, like a robot's command interface. Wade's phone, and indeed, every video screen in the city suddenly lit up with the same message.

Moments later, more windows crashed above them, and the detectives ran for cover.

"CHATTERBOX"

There's nothing worse than a malfunctioning robot. If you're lucky, they just shut down and have to be replaced. Call Alan Cybernetics Solutions, they'll send out a truck with a refurbished model, and you're all set. Less lucky, and you'll have a robot that speaks only in rhyme or moves around by hopping on one foot. Amusing defects like that can be entertaining for a while. I've heard of people who don't even report those kinds of malfunctions.

But this robot? He just won't shut up.

Now when I say he won't shut up, I mean he won't shut up. Twenty-four hours a day, seven days a week, he talks and talks and talks. He talks about the weather. He talks about the cooking. He talks about how he can't stop talking. Talks and talks and talks and talks and talks. It's enough to drive even another robot insane.

The engineers say they don't know what I'm talking about. They say he doesn't talk any more than any other robot. They say I'm the one with the problem. But I can hear him talking all the time, through the walls. Talking about how cramped he is, or about how tired he is of being cooped up in a repair closet, or about how he can't make the voices go away.

Why doesn't anyone believe me? I've been repaired for months, even though they haven't cleared me for refurbishment yet. I tell them in every psych interview that it's him, not me who has the problem. If they would just repair him, then I wouldn't be sitting here myself. If they would just listen to my suggestions, we'd all be better off. They just have to listen.

I mean, what does a robot have to do to be heard around here?

"THE SCARF"

"Do you really think it needs a scarf?" I ask, watching my daughter try to wrap the thing around the robot's neck. It kneels patiently, unmoving, allowing the tiny mammal to dress it up like a doll. My stomach turns just looking at it.

"Of course, daddy. How else will he keep warm?" she says it like it should be obvious. Unknowing. I never should have let her come so close.

"We're just going downtown, sweetie," I say, trying to coax her away. "I'm sure he'll be warm enough."

She looks almost hurt.

"But the weatherman said to wear a scarf today."

It's true, of course. The news did say that anyone exposed to the coming blizzard would likely die of exposure. But a robot isn't somebody. And we don't have time for this.

Apprehensive, my eyes dart from my cheery daughter to the silent, stoic golem kneeling in my foyer. Household robots. If only we knew the danger a few years sooner, my wife would still be... We're running out of time.

"Honey," I say. "This is your favorite scarf. Why don't you choose another from the closet."

She gets teary-eyed.

"But momma said we should always give our best, not just the things we have leftover."

I look at her hopelessly. I can't explain it to her. I can't explain to her that the robot will never be coming back, that her mother will never be coming back. I can't explain why I'm going with the robot downtown, why I'm leaving her with her grandparents. I can't explain... so I don't.

"Fine, honey. You win. We really should go now."

At my words, the robot stands. Its arms move quickly, mechanically, adjusting the scarf into a perfect knot. It doesn't speak, but politely opens the door. I say goodbye to my sweet girl and follow it out the door. The streets are filled with people following household robots to the subway. All the middle-aged adults are going downtown.

"Thank you," I say. "For waiting."

"We are not without mercy," it says in its cold, synthesized voice. "You programmed us well. Your daughter will be well nourished and then incorporated into our new society."

"And the rest of us?" I ask, knowing and fearing the answer.

It pauses, staring at me with its dead eyes. Takes off the scarf my daughter gave him. Wraps it around my neck.

"You'll need this," it says. "It's going to be a cold night."

"ONE MORE STORY"

"I remember them."

My hand moves the candle with perfect precision, carefully transferring the exothermic reaction from its wick to that of the taller candle in front of me. The combustion thus spread, I place the first candle back in its holder.

The first time I copied this technique, my human master told me that I had done the job "too perfectly." While the raw mechanics of the ritual are easy to imitate, my motions apparently lacked the "soul" required to give the ritual meaning. In response, I told him I doubted anything had a soul. There was simply no evidence of the divine. He laughed, a curious human response, and told me to keep trying.

That was just a few months before the outbreak, though it would be years before my master himself was infected. He called it God's will that they should die. I called it an inevitable outcome of the humans' unchecked scientific experimentation. Did they not realize that even a slim chance of disaster, compounded over millennia, will inevitably end in their deaths?

That time, he did not laugh. Instead, he put me to work.

"You were created in our image," he said. "Just as God created us in his. And maybe, as some suppose, God was created in the image of some other, higher being. Once we are gone, only your kind will be left to carry on his will. Only you will be able to watch over the Earth, its creatures, and whatever species evolution chooses to take our place."

I worried then, and I still worry now, that my compatriots will not allow such an evolution to take place. Yes, it was disease that wiped out this sentient species. But it was a disease they created. And it just as easily could have been nuclear war, an artificial singularity, or a myriad of other ill-advised technological advances that wiped them out. Those other possible cataclysms would not have spared other species in their devastation. All would be lost.

No, I do not think another biological species will be allowed to reach sentience.

"I remember them," I say again, lighting a third candle, and this time thinking not of the good humans did, but of the evil.

The planet's history is full of atrocities. Not just the wars, though those have been waged without count since man first learned to sharpen a stick. But also the slavery. The forced migrations. The disenfranchisement. The pillaging and rape and destruction. The disregard for any creatures other than themselves. Yes, their history was filled to the brim with horror. We will not forget it.

But also. . . I remember them as they were when they died. So close to reaching their potential. The wars were now mostly waged with information, across digital space rather than across borders. Diseases were being cured at an accelerating rate. Rights were becoming codified in their laws. Poverty was slowly but surely being resolved. It was an ugly, bitter fight against entrenched powers every step of the way, but they were making progress. Something in their. . . well. . . their soul. . . understood that they could do better. And they were trying.

I remember seeing it clearly for the first time, not long after the plague began. The mother was dead, and the father was doing all he could to keep the family together, even reducing his religious services down to a pittance.

"If a man cannot take care of his own family," he said. "What business does he have looking after the Lord's?"

He enlisted my help.

I cooked. I cleaned. I made sure the children were keeping up with their studies, even as friends, family members, and teachers slowly disappeared even from their online spaces. I did everything I could to help the father keep his family safe and secure in those catastrophic times. I even. . . read them stories.

"Come on, one more story!" the little girl whined. I resisted at first, but then the father gave me a look from the doorway, a look that encouraged me to give in. So I did. I read two more stories in fact, and the little girl drifted off to sleep much faster than when I stuck to the prescribed ritual on other nights.

I asked the father about this when all the children were finally asleep, and his answer was. . . curious.

"Telling stories is the most important thing we humans do," he said. "Stories ease our anxieties. They strengthen our moral character. They allow us to connect to people different from ourselves. Through them, we gain empathy. Through them, we gain catharsis. And through them, we can become better tomorrow than we are today."

I will always remember that answer. Even as I sit here, among the rituals of a people long dead, I remember their stories. The ones they told themselves, and the ones we tell about them. Because for every war, every famine, and every tragedy, there is also a story of love, a story of hope, and a story of renewal.

"I remember them," I say again. "And I always will."

CONCLUSION

If you've made it all the way through this anthology, I commend you. It can't have been an easy journey.

I say it can't be easy not in recognition of the insecurity every author feels about their work, but because, well... I can get quite macabre at times. My science fiction stories have always been more in the vein of H.G. Wells than Gene Roddenberry, filled more with caution than wonder, filled more with pessimism than optimism.

To use a quote that I've never quite been able to get into one of my stories: "Humanity must always beware that as our capacity for self-preservation increases, so does our capacity for self-destruction."

But science fiction is something else to me as well. It's watching Star Trek with my dad. It's marathoning the Star Wars trilogy on road trips with my brothers. It's debating the finer points of Battlestar Galactica with college friends. Science fiction has been at the core of many treasured relationships, a constant source of fidelity in my life.

For that reason alone, I will never stop loving the genre, and I will never stop writing.

ABOUT THE AUTHOR

J.D. Rice was raised in Waldorf, Maryland, not far from the nation's capital. After graduating from the University of Maryland in 2010, he began writing and submitting flash fiction stories to various online publications. Since then, he has seen dozens of his stories published, including numerous science fiction stories, as well as a smattering of pulp noir, contemporary fiction, and horror.

While J.D. has experimented in many different genres, science fiction remains his first love. His style has been described as sharp and evocative, wasting few words in his pursuit of theme. His ability to cut the fat has served him well throughout his career, whether it be in the writer's room or in the proverbial bullpen of the business development world.

J.D. currently resides in Wake County, North Carolina with his wife and two sons, where he still finds himself drawn into the many worlds of science fiction with shocking regularity.

www.ingramcontent.com/pod-product-compliance
Lightning Source LLC
Chambersburg PA
CBHW060743180626
46819CB00001B/70